Snail
and
Slug

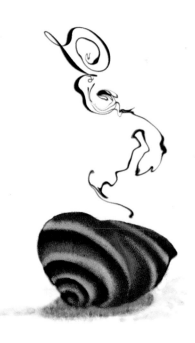

Snail

atheneum

A Richard Jackson Book

Atheneum Books for Young Readers • New York London Toronto Sydney New Delhi

Slug and

written and illustrated by
Denys Cazet

atheneum

ATHENEUM BOOKS FOR YOUNG READERS
An imprint of Simon & Schuster Children's Publishing Division
1230 Avenue of the Americas, New York, New York 10020
Copyright © 2016 by Denys Cazet
ATHENEUM BOOKS FOR YOUNG READERS is a registered trademark of Simon & Schuster, Inc.
Atheneum logo is a trademark of Simon & Schuster, Inc.
For information about special discounts for bulk purchases, please contact Simon & Schuster Special Sales at 1-866-506-1949 or business@simonandschuster.com.
The Simon & Schuster Speakers Bureau can bring authors to your live event. For more information or to book an event, contact the Simon & Schuster Speakers Bureau at 1-866-248-3049 or visit our website at www.simonspeakers.com.
Book design by Lauren Rille
The text for this book is set in Hardwood.
The illustrations for this book are rendered in mixed media.
Manufactured in China
0216 SCP
First Edition
10 9 8 7 6 5 4 3 2 1
CIP data for this book is available from the Library of Congress.
ISBN 978-1-4814-4506-1
ISBN 978-1-4814-4507-8 (eBook)

For Sandy Baxter,
a much belated thank-you

SNAIL SAT IN THE cool shade by the edge of a small creek.

"Whew!" she said. "It's hot today."

"Tell me about it!" said Slug. "Any hotter and I'd look like I'd been sizzled in a bowl of salt!"

Snail looked around. "Where are you?"
"Up here," called Slug. "Under this leaf."
Slug peeked out. "At least you have a
house to crawl into. Look at me. Nothing.
I don't even have a pocket!"

Snail felt sorry for Slug.

"Would you like to come into my house for a cold drink?"

Slug stared at Snail's shell. "Yes," she said. "But . . ."

Snail smiled. "Oh, don't worry, my house is bigger than it looks."

Snail pulled in her head. She pulled in her tail. "Come on in," she called. "The door is open."

Snail was waiting in the kitchen.
"Please," she said. "Sit down."
Snail poured some iced tea into two tall glasses.

"Cheers," said Snail.   "Cheers," said Slug.

"Your house *is* bigger than it looks," Slug remarked.
"You can't always judge a book by its cover," said Snail.
She put the empty glasses in the dishwasher.

In the living room, Snail and Slug sat on a cozy sofa.

Slug noticed a picture on the wall. "Who is that?" she asked.

"Oh!" said Snail. "That was Mr. Snail. He was eaten by a robin."

 Slug gasped. "Oh! I'm so sorry."

"Yes," replied Snail. "You just never know."

"No, you never do. Mr. Slug was eaten by a toad."

"This is my bedroom," said Snail.
"I like it dark and damp."
"Me too," agreed Slug.

Snail showed Slug another bedroom.
"Do you like the wallpaper?" Snail asked.
"I glued it myself."
"Lovely," said Slug.

"And this is the library," Snail announced. "Do you have a favorite book?"

"I'm not a very good reader," Slug admitted. "But . . . I'm a great cook!"

"I'm not a very good cook," confessed Snail. "But I'm a very good reader."

"I saw some water lettuce by the creek," said Slug. "I'll make you lunch."

"We'll go on a picnic!" said Snail. She took a picnic basket out of the cupboard. "After lunch, I'll read you a story."

"Wait here," she said, opening another door. "I'll be right back!"
"Where are you going?"
"To the cellar. We need something nice to drink."

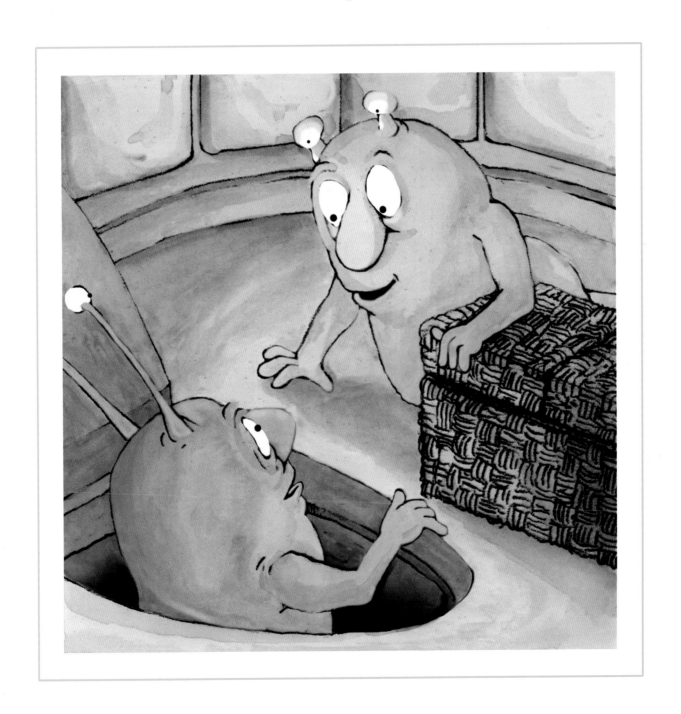

Snail and Slug sat on a mossy rock by the edge of the creek.
Slug looked at Snail.
"What is it?" Snail asked.
"When you are out of your house," said Slug, "you look like me."
"We must be cousins," said Snail.

Slug opened the picnic basket. *"Oh!"*
"Slug! What's wrong?"
"There's a salt shaker in there!"
"I know. Be careful," warned Snail.

Slug picked some water lettuce and put it in a bowl.

While she added a little of this and a little of that, she sang a salad song:

> "I'm making a salad,
> While singing a ballad
> For my new friend Snail and me.
> The song is delicious,
> The salad nutritious,
> May I pour you some red-berry tea?"

"Very nice," said Snail.

"It would be better with a piano," suggested Slug. "Salad?"

"Please," said Snail. "It looks yummy!"

"It does!" snarled a big banana slug.
His name was Four Eyes.
"What do you want?" Snail asked.
"Your lettuce or your life!" growled Four Eyes.

He pinched Snail.

"Gimme it or you'll be the first to go, Snail!"

"No!" begged Snail. "Please, no!"

Slug reached into the picnic basket and pulled out the salt shaker.
"Leave Snail alone!" she demanded.

Four Eyes glared at Slug. "What is that?"

"It's a salt shaker!" cried Slug. "And I'm not afraid to use it!"

Four Eyes scoffed. "Ha! I don't believe you!"

Slug sprinkled a little salt on Four Eyes's tail.
His tail began to fizz, and his bottom began to foam.

He jumped into the creek

and wiggled in the cool water.

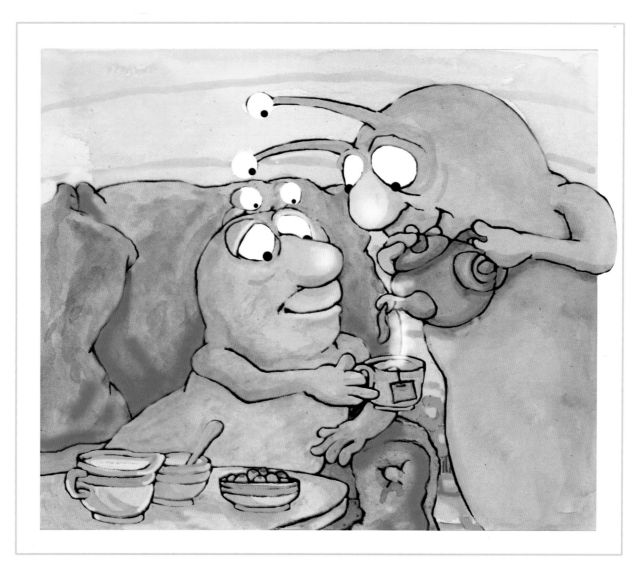

The two new friends sat in Snail's living room.
Snail served red-berry tea.
"You were very brave," she said.
"Oh . . . ," said Slug. "That's what friends do."
"Slug, may I ask you something?"
"Of course."

"Well . . . my house is big. . . . And you don't even have a pocket. . . .
I was wondering . . . would you like to share my house?"

"May I do the cooking?"

"Every day!" said Snail. "After dinner, I'll read you a story."

"And after that," said Slug, "I'll sing you a new song."

"And play the piano!" added Snail.

Slug looked around the room.

"Snail," she said, "I don't see a piano."

"Upstairs," said Snail. "In the attic."